'They had no choice'

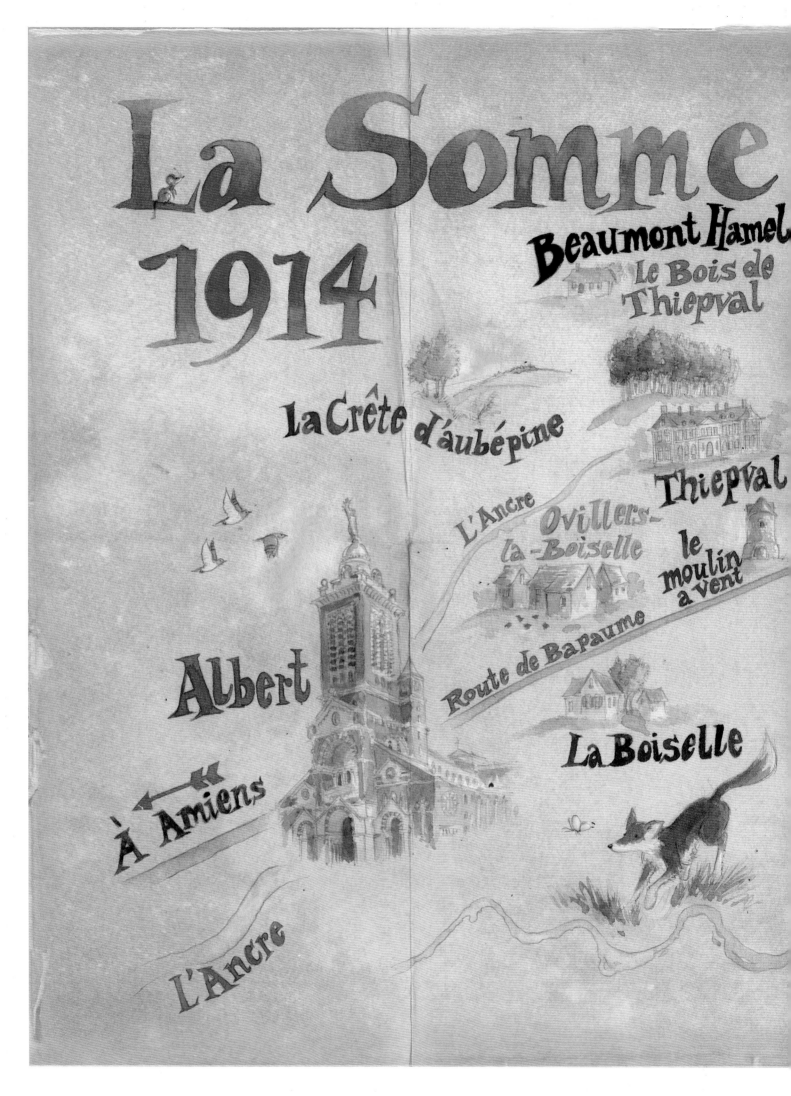

In memory of my grandpa,
who served with the Royal Engineers during World War 1
and thereafter as an Inspector for the RSPCA.

HR

For my dad.

MI

first edition

STRAUSS HOUSE PRODUCTIONS
www.strausshouseproductions.com

First published in Great Britain 2015
British Library Cataloguing in Publication Data
A catalogue record for this book is available from the British Library

FLO of the Somme

by
Hilary Robinson & Martin Impey

STRAUSS HOUSE
PRODUCTIONS

These are the dogs that saved lives.

This is Flo, a hero of war,
A mercy dog that saved lives.

This is Ray with the Medical Corps,
Who served with Flo, a hero of war,
A mercy dog that saved lives.

This is the pigeon, shot in the wing,
That flew through danger in order to bring
A message for Ray and the Medical Corps,
Who served with Flo, a hero of war,
A mercy dog that saved lives.

Here's the medical kit that was sent
Out with Flo from the hospital tent,
After the pigeon, shot in the wing,
Flew through danger in order to bring
A message for Ray and the Medical Corps,
Who served with Flo, a hero of war,
A mercy dog that saved lives.

This is the battlefield Flo ran over,
A field of bullets where once was clover,
Complete with medical kit that was sent
Out with her from the hospital tent,
After the pigeon, shot in the wing,
Flew through danger in order to bring
A message for Ray and the Medical Corps,
Who served with Flo, a hero of war,
A mercy dog that saved lives.

This is the donkey running with Ray
Out to where the injured lay,
Across the battlefield Flo ran over,
A field of bullets where once was clover,
Complete with medical kit that was sent
Out with her from the hospital tent,
After the pigeon, shot in the wing,
Flew through danger in order to bring
A message for Ray and the Medical Corps,
Who served with Flo, a hero of war,
A mercy dog that saved lives.

This is the wood Ray ran through
On hearing the bark of a dog who knew
A donkey was running along with Ray
Out to where the injured lay,
Across the battlefield Flo ran over,
A field of bullets where once was clover,
Complete with medical kit that was sent
Out with her from the hospital tent,
After the pigeon, shot in the wing,
Flew through danger in order to bring
A message for Ray and the Medical Corps,
Who served with Flo, a hero of war,
A mercy dog that saved lives.

Here's Crucifix Corner Flo stood by,
A beacon in a stormy sky,
Near the wood that Ray ran through
On hearing the bark of a dog who knew
A donkey was running along with Ray
Out to where the injured lay,
Across the battlefield Flo ran over,
A field of bullets where once was clover,
Complete with medical kit that was sent
Out with her from the hospital tent,
After the pigeon, shot in the wing,
Flew through danger in order to bring
A message for Ray and the Medical Corps,
Who served with Flo, a hero of war,
A mercy dog that saved lives.

These are the pilots she found.

These are the pilots Flo found
Next to their planes, shot to the ground,
Near the place that she stood by,
That beacon in the stormy sky,
Near the wood that Ray ran through
On hearing the bark of a dog who knew
A donkey was running along with Ray
Out to where the injured lay,
Across the battlefield Flo ran over,
A field of bullets where once was clover,
Complete with medical kit that was sent
Out with her from the hospital tent,
After the pigeon, shot in the wing,
Flew through danger in order to bring
A message for Ray and the Medical Corps,
Who served with Flo, a hero of war,
A mercy dog that...

...saved lives.

'Treat me well - I have done my bit.'

Image © M.IMPEY 2015 - Animals In War Memorial - Brook Gate, Park Lane, London, England.

Over 50,000 dogs, more than 100,000 pigeons
and approximately 8,000,000 horses and mules along with
elephants, camels, cats, goats, canaries, bears, a baboon,
a springbok, a golden eagle, a fox, rabbits, chickens
and even glow-worms were used on all sides during World War One.

'THEY HAD NO CHOICE'

Thank you
Jackie Hamley, Jim Millea, Megan Brownrigg, Gary Brandham, Joke de Winter,
Nerys Spofforth, Cathi Poole, Nicky Stonehill, Jessica Ward, Dan Purvis, Helen Nicholson,
Paul Reed (ww1revisited.com), Robin Schäfer (gottmituns.net), Betty Bennison, Damian Leese
and always a very special *'Thank you'* to Andrew Robinson and Emilie James.
Last, but by no means least, thanks to the *'real Flo'* aka Kibo Tapp!

Also by
Hilary Robinson & Martin Impey

Praise for Where The Poppies Now Grow

"... a poignant yet hopeful story of how friendship endures the hardest of times and provides an accessible route into considering the First World War."
Carolyn Swain - The English Association

"...children will never look at poppies in the same way again."
Paul Reed - Military Historian

"...a powerful and beautifully written poem, superbly illustrated, one which touches our hearts."
Gervase Phinn - Bestselling Author

"...a book that reflects the lasting importance of both friendship and place and how they can help to heal the tragedy of war."
Julia Eccleshare MBE - Lovereading 4 kids

ISBN - 978-0-9571245-8-5

ISBN - 978-0-9571245-7-8

Praise for The Christmas Truce

"Hilary Robinson and Martin Impey beautifully weave poetry and illustration to retell the poignant story of The Christmas Truce."
Seven Stories - National Centre for Children's Books

"...splendidly retold and beautifully illustrated."
Robin Schäfer - Military Historian (Germany)

"This truly is a brilliant book with such a positive message of peace emerging from such a terrible and tragic conflict."
Readitdaddy.blogspot.co.uk

"...'The Christmas Truce' is a delightful rhyme about the First World War...Both books highlight the human qualities that all people share, despite the tragedy and destruction associated with combat."
The Western Front Association

ISBN - 978-0-9571245-5-4

For more information about Strauss House Productions
www.strausshouseproductions.com

'Like us' on Facebook - Where The Poppies Now Grow